Almost Everyone Dies in the End

Stories by First Year Seminar Students
at Southwestern University

Fall 2013

ISBN: 1494346583
ISBN-13: 978-1494346584

CONTENTS

ACKNOWLEDGMENTS

Many thanks to President Edward Burger and Provost Jim Hunt for their support of Creative Writing and the First Year Seminar Program at Southwestern University. And special gratitude is due to Julie Cowley for her guidance, to Paige Guerra for the use of her original cover art "Sharp and Dull," and to Dana Hendrix, Kathryn Stallard, and the library staff in the Special Collections of the A. Frank Smith Jr. Library for providing the invaluable, tangible resources that helped inspire many of the stories here.

INTRODUCTION

The short stories collected here were written in the fall of 2013 by freshmen Southwestern University students enrolled in a First Year Seminar devoted to exploring the sub-genre of creative writing sometimes called flash fiction, micro fiction, or the short-short story. Telling a clear and compelling story is a difficult business, and these students faced the additional challenge of conveying their narratives in a compressed form, making use of no more than 400 to 750 words. In order to capture character, plot, setting and theme in so limited a space—while still preserving a central vision—the writers were compelled to strip away unessential details, sometimes distilling the story's essence, sometimes offering a brief glimpse of a much larger story that unfolds beyond the margins of the page. The title of the collection, *Almost Everyone Dies in the End*, comes from a workshop discussion during the last week of the course, in which the class realized that for most of their characters—as for a great number of fictional characters—things do not turn out very well. We hope readers will find these stories engaging and entertaining.

John Pipkin
Writer-in-Residence
Southwestern University
Georgetown, Texas 2013

AND OFF IT WENT

Denisse Ayala

Her name was Eugenia. She burned two things. One of them being a book, the other her husband. Bernardo Francisco De Montemayor Cordova, a fine believer in the Divine Right of Kings, obtained the characteristic of "machismo" from past generations. King Charles II dominated the throne and De Montemayor Cordova was his right hand man. The king asked him to write the bylaws of the nation and publish them for future generations of Spain. But, you see, every king has his secrets, and De

Montemayor Cordova did not mention those within the bylaws. Women didn't have rights, and religion was imposed on everyone. It was believed that the king had been granted the right to establish right from wrong by a higher being or God, and Eugenia Quiroga De Montemayor believed the contrary.

As Eugenia watched her "beloved" husband finish up the book, her face unconsciously wrinkled into an expression of aversion at the mere thought of its content. Agony and murderous rage filled her head with thoughts of finishing them both off. She set her husband's work aside and prepared him dinner, just as a good wife should. He treated her with disgust, spit out her dinner, and took advantage of the only womanhood she had, again. He dragged her to the back of the room. Her hands rough and deteriorated, from second-degree burns while cooking and the arduous act of hand-washing his clothing; however, this time it wasn't the labor that caused Eugenia's hands to bleed. Her nails scratching into the moldy wooden floor screeched loudly.

Sickened with fear, she ignored her bloody hands and listened to the screech as he dragged her in. She cried out, she felt her breathe jerking back and forth in her lungs, as if he were stabbing her without mercy. She could hear again. He left her sitting on the floor and she wept hysterically. She did nothing, said nothing, felt nothing, nothing but emptiness. When the day of the printing came, she took action.

His agonizing screams were heard from their humble abode, the heavy scent of his burning flesh permeated through everyone's nostrils from a mile away, but Eugenia was not there. She was printing her husband's book. She thanked Canterella for putting her "beloved" husband into a deep slumber right before the incident and dressed up for *La Tomatina*. Eugenia's face showed no sorrow, agony, or guilt. She would've dressed in colored clothing for *La Tomatina*, king's orders. However, her black clothing spoke for her as she displayed no expression. As King Charles II arrived at *La Tomatina*, he acknowledged Eugenia's loss and offered words of compassion. Her only response was a request for a ceremonial mourning in honor of her husband's death.

The following morning, all townsfolk arrived in their best wear, not knowing what to expect. The king wore his best attire, in respect of Spain's loss. Upon arriving, Eugenia didn't speak, for her actions were enough. With the light of a match, she burned the bylaws of the nation to a crisp. King Charles II, astonished by her act, reacted with a simple, yet very important line… off with her head and off her head went.

ANXIETY

Emma Barnebey

You have crash landed on an alien planet. At first, this planet seems just like your own. The aliens look just like the people back home, and even speak the same language. You are given a home just like on Earth. You feel safe in the familiarity. Despite this, though, you still want to get back home—but the damage to your ship is difficult to fix, keeping you here for the time being.

Then things around you start to change. You get nervous about things that no one else gets nervous about. That sense of safety drops away and your back hurts from the tension that strikes you more and more frequently. It gets harder to fall asleep at night because there's an awful tightness in your chest, and your head hurts a lot of the time.

Sometimes it's hard to breathe, and you come to the conclusion that there must be something in this air that you're not used to. It starts to mess with your mind and now the reason you're not falling asleep is that you start going over every little bad thing you've ever done in your life until your brain wears itself out. That makes you cranky the next day, which makes you do more bad things, and that gives you even more to worry over.

Now you feel a certain paranoia every time you go out. You are terrified of messing up because you know you'll agonize over it, so usually you just observe. It's like all of your flaws are under a magnifying glass, but you keep quiet in the hopes that no one else will look through it. The aliens seem totally unaffected by this unseen evil you're so constantly aware of. You wonder if this is really something you can't control, since everyone around you controls it so well. Maybe you're just weak, or maybe you just have bigger flaws than they do, and that's why you think about them so often.

Finally, you can't take it anymore, and decide to do whatever it takes to repair your ship. The aliens offer you instruction manuals based on ships they've seen before, because they are genuinely concerned about your condition. You are constantly paranoid that you're really just an annoyance they want gone. You probably are. You definitely are.
None of the instructions work—the ones you had with you don't tell you anything and the ones the aliens have are informative but have nothing to do with your ship. You get frustrated and feel like a failure, which is something else to worry about. Eventually, fixing your ship starts to seem impossible. You try to console yourself and think that perhaps you will build up an immunity to this strange toxin someday—if not, well, you'll just take the stress day by day.

You probably deserve to go crazy, anyway.

BRANDED

Amanda *Blanchard*

I lay at their feet, afraid and hopeless. I could feel bruises forming all over my body and a mixture of sweat and blood run down my forehead. The summer sun shone fiercely down onto the plantation, casting large shadows on the gravel of the men surrounding me. Two of them grabbed me by my arms and forced me to stand. My coarse, black hands were then tied tightly onto the wooden fence post in front of me. They threatened me with my life if I were to dare make a sound. Out of the corner of my eye, I watched a white man dressed in fine linens approach the men and me. In his right hand, he held a smoldering iron rod, with the initial 'T' shaped out on one end. My body began to quiver as I heard the rocks crunch under his boots from behind me. "Get ready to live the rest of your life in pain you worthless nigger!" With that, he dug the iron brand into my shoulder blade, filling the air with the smell of burning flesh.

Forty-eight years later, my body is still labeled with William Tucker's seal of ownership. Although now, it no longer symbolizes ownership, but rather a time in history that mankind will forever be ashamed of. By the grace of God, I eventually managed to make a life for myself, one with a family, property, and a business. My little piece of land overlooks a large cattle ranch. Sometimes, in the mornings, I like to sit on the back porch and watch the cows graze freely. However, today, the ranchers have herded the cattle together in the middle of the field. I watch from afar as they lasso a newborn baby calf out of the group, separating it from its mother. With ropes locked around its neck and its hind legs, they bring it to the ground. The ropes are pulled tightly in opposite directions, stretching the calf's body to keep it from thrashing about. A man in a black cowboy hat approaches the calf, kneels before it, and digs a smoking, hot iron brand into its backside. My skin cringes as the calf bellows a loud, heart-wrenching noise. Its days like this when I wonder if man will forever be guilty of slavery.

THE END

JD Bornstad

We never left each other's side in the midst of warfare. As we ran through the trenches, crossfire whizzed inches from our helmets. Clumps of dirt flew up in our sights as metal fragments from grenades and heavy artillery hit in our proximity. With my younger brother and I being the last standing from our squad, we were retreating for our own survival. Our numbers were slowly dropping one by one as the firefight took its course, but at this point my brother and I surviving to see the light of tomorrow was the only thing that mattered.

We were surrounded; ammunition running scarce as we unloaded each clip and reloaded another magazine; I would be lying if I said I wasn't scared. With my back against the sandbags, my mind began to run and jump to the conclusion that in a matter of seconds my life will soon end. I turned to look at my brother; he turned to me as well. As we locked eyes, we both knew we were thinking our lives were approaching the same conclusion. While I was tearing up, I grabbed my brother's hand and began to state what was my final goodbye to him:

"You're my hero little bro. You're all I got and I am right here with you 'til the end.

He grabbed the back of my helmet and placed his helmet against mine and said:

"I love you too big guy; now let's give 'em hell."

We both stood up and turned at the same time to face the Germans. I clenched the trigger as bullets took flight. My assault rifle soon ran out of ammo and before I had time to wield my pistol, I was jerked back by the impact of burning hot metal entering my torso. I landed on my back with unbearable pain and shortness of breath. Blood slowly began to fill my mouth, which inhibited my ability to speak. Lying there, I turned to the sight of my brother not moving; not breathing; possessing a stone cold face. Tears soon rolled down my face; but shortly after I began to lose feeling in that. As the pain began to fade, my sight was slowly giving away as everything around me turned to black. As my life was ending, I accepted my fate knowing that I had the brother I loved more than anything by my side.

FOURTH OF JULY

John De Luna

I remember it like it was only yesterday, the smoky grey sky, and the grass was covered in flames, and I lying down in the center of the remaining rumble from my house. It was the morning before Fourth of July; my parents were on a four-day cruise in the Bahamas and I was stuck at home taking care of my two younger brothers, Clemente and Miguel.

I wasn't too fond in looking after my brothers but I realized that it would be a great experience to spend quality time with them. We started by playing our favorite video game, Super Smash Bros., my brother bickering about who was better than the other one like always. It was great that I got to just chill with my brothers and have a good time doing pretty much whatever we wanted to do. It was around eleven o'clock, close to midnight and the clouds had completely covered the sky.

An earsplitting explosion-like sound roofed throughout the house. My brothers startled, I took a peek moving the curtains in order to see what had happened. As I looked, once again there was another explosion but this time I saw it was a combination of fireworks and lightning. The people started to celebrate a bit too early but the more fireworks I saw the more lightning was coming down. Until finally something usual happened. The lightning struck the gargantuan oak tree in front of our house and it was coming down rapidly in flames. The sight of a burning tree gave a sick feeling in my stomach and the screams of my brothers didn't help me think straight. I couldn't move as if I was paralyzed until the tree collided with the right side of the house.

Finally I could move again, my brothers were running around me in complete terror and the house had caught on fire entirely. Trapped in the living room we were all surrounded by smoke, ashes, and flaming furniture. I quickly thought to go through the window but was blocked by a wave of flames. I saw the game controllers on the floor; I grabbed and launched them to the window, shattering it to pieces. I could now hear the sirens of the fire trucks coming closer but the fire grew bigger now. As I looked to my brothers, I saw their innocent scared faces and told them that everything thing was going to be fine as long as they trusted me. They nodded. I told Clemente to jump through the window, so he did. I grabbed Miguel, kissed him on his forehead and tossed him through the window. As I got ready to leap outside, the whole building collapsed and well I was looking down at the scene. My brothers running towards the firefighters safely and the house still up in flames as the rain came down.

Happy 4th of July.

ALL THAT GLITTERS

Rebecca Dowlearn

I walk down corridors where molds of chiseled abs and hourglass figures line the halls, anticipation drumming around my hollow stomach. Today I am meeting with Dr. Ralph Jenkins, an experimental beauty consultant at the forefront of the fashion industry. Testimonies of his success glare strikingly from the front covers of fashion magazines only to evaporate from the fashion world, transformed. When I reach Ralph's office we shake hands and size each other up. This is the man who claims to have the power to fix me. I am what he has to work with.

His eyes calculate the effort it will take, and for a moment I don't know if I should be here.

"Lily Jordan. It looks like I have your signed liability waiver, so why don't we get started," he says and steadies me with a smile.

I lay on a metal table in an empty room that engulfs me in bright, scrutinizing light. The first team of specialists arrive and promptly begin their work. They strip me of unflattering hair and correct my washed-out skin with a golden tan spray. Afterwards a woman from the team paints over and around the features of my face like a blank canvas. When she is done she holds up a mirror in front of me. My face, once uninspiring and unsearched, now looks open and inviting. I have innocent, sparkling doe eyes and full, luscious lips. I can already picture strangers staring in awe and hanging onto my every word. People are going to know that I am important.

Another team puts me under to begin the next phase of my transformation. While I sleep they cut at my body, taking away fat and adding curves in all the right places. The aftermath is painful, but I rejoice to say good riddance to my old graceless body, a body that always felt intrusive. My new body is still short and somewhat stubby, but as Ralph promised, the last phase of my transformation, limb and neck elongation, is going to fix all of this.

The last team walks in donning scrubs, followed by a line of photographers. Ralph explains to me excitedly that I'm going to be a "big deal". I have turned into one of his greatest works, maybe even his masterpiece. For this last phase, I am given medicine to numb and immobilize my body. Before I can wonder why they don't put me under I hear the snaps as they dislocate my limbs. Ralph never intended for me to leave, I realize, and now neither does my body. First I have willowy arms, and next I have graceful legs. A man steps behind my head and in my peripheral vision I watch his hands take hold of my neck. For a moment I think his hands are reverent, but they are just executing. There is one last snap, and I am engulfed in bright, adoring flashes of light. I hadn't prepared myself for death, but I'm lucky that I end like this.

I am perfect.

I am beautiful.

I am treasured.

THE AXE

Anne Finch

When I am a very young girl I hear for the first time the story of how my mother first killed a man. She whispers it in my ear like a bedtime story. She considers the deed more of an exchange than a murder; he took everything from her, so she took his axe and his life. She keeps the axe, still caked with blood, above the entrance to our home. She whispers that one day it will be mine.

At the age of thirteen I still have this air of mystique attached to my mother. My peers, all teenagers like me, have grown disillusioned with the women who gave them life. They have begun to see the cracks in the once-flawless image of parental power. Their guardians are no longer gods; they are people, people who hold over them an absolute control they find unbearable.

I, however, idolize my mother, and fear her. Her power is earned, and absolute. She is everything to me; she is my only guardian. Every time I ask her about my father's identity, or his fate, her eyes drift to the bloodied axe above the doorway.

I stop asking.

At sixteen, I bring home a boy, an empty-headed yet burly and handsome lad I'd met in town. However, the moment I pull him across the doorway to our home, I feel strange, as if something in the air has shifted. I look almost expectantly at the familiar heirloom only to see something I've never seen before: the axe is missing.

I unceremoniously remove the boy with little explanation, making a hasty promise to see him again soon, at his home instead of mine. My mother makes no mention of the incident with the axe, and as always, I follow her example. However, when I mention the boy I've met she swells up, like an angry cat. I learn not to mention him, yet continue to see him secretly. I quietly navigate my own road between the man I begin to trust implicitly and the unyielding pillar that is my only guardian. She trusts me too much to suspect.

At eighteen I stumble home, wiping my blood from my hands and face onto my torn dress. I can feel bruises starting to materialize, but beneath those something even greater is forming; my own rage. I hate this boy for everything he's done to me, for everything I let him do to me: the way he coerced me, pitted me against myself, for making me believe for a second that the exterior and interior damage he's caused is even partly my own doing. In this moment, I am so blindly angry I understand everything.

I understand. And I am ready.

My blood continues to ooze from the cuts and

sores he has etched into my body, streaking across my face and my hands and my dress. I ignore it, and I smile widely as for the first time I reach for my mother's axe.

WEI T'O

Sam Guess

I am tending to my cattle when the flash hits. I shield my eyes and look away to my wife and our two boys on the porch of my home. Heat incinerates everything I see before I feel it swept through my flesh. Fog floods around me and I cry out, my voice choking on sorrow. I hear nothing as each word I scream is swallowed into the abyss beyond the fog. They must all be out there, lost and hopeless. I have to help them. I must do something but my every motion feels so challenging. The haze is changing, becoming darker and colder and weighs on my chest.

With each gasp I can move less until I am stuck in place.

My eyes fall and I see it again, my cattle, my home, my family, all illuminated by a flash and then engulfed in flames. The image runs through my mind again and again. I know I must have passed on, but these thoughts hurt as if I were living. Sweat rolls off my brow and I surmise the cruelty displayed by the belly of flames being so dark. It had been such a beautiful day; I see it all so clearly. The air was warm and running through the hills of my farmland outside of Hiroshima. My wife was telling stories while helping the boys build kites. I tended to our cattle, basking in the laughter of my children. With this memory a smile pulls at my face and I collapse as the weight surrounding me lifts. I open my eyes to witness light panning through the fog. It clears a trail through the haze which I begin to drift along.

A golden figure stands at the end of my path and blocks the entry of a massive gate. He bows and introduces himself as Wei T'o, guardian of the next life. He explains to me that my memories of love cleared the fog to illuminate the way to his gate, but my work is not done. And in order to enter the next life I must balance the fog with the light. I must balance my fear with my love. He says in doing this I will leave all I have experienced behind, forgotten but saved in the afterlife. Only then, Wei T'o explains, will I be ready.

J.D. TUCKER

Nyokabi Kamau

"How's this?" Bonnie's voice is a sweet southern chime in the quiet November air. Sun light begged to touch her skin as she turned her chin downward, gracefully extending her right arm. The red robe on her slender silhouette hung in delicate creases. Pompously she stood, for the world belonged to her. "This has to be perfect."

The young Negro was possessed with crazed artistic spasms, medicated only by the blank canvas before him. She didn't normally let Negros paint her, but his undiscovered hand was exceptional. She licked her lips promiscuously when the two made eye contact. The black figure secretly smirked. He tries to hide it but the love he has for her almost crushes through the painting as the strokes began to bleed into each other.

"Of course madam," was all he could murmur, consumed by the fabric on her shoulder that dropped ever so slightly.

"Where's my tea!"

A Negro maid glides over to Bonnie's plea immediately and hands her an ivory cup. Now the maid was a thick rather quirky, dark woman whose glances and smiles at the Negro lasted far too long, and who Bonnie undoubtedly detested. For this, the maid always exited with silent haste.

However the man was entranced. By now he was immersed in Bonnie's beauty, drinking in her blonde hair, swimming in the pool of blue that were her eyes. Bonnie laughed at the way his view shifted nervously and proceeded to walk over to the black chiseled creature in slow, measured steps across the hay cluttered ground.

"But-", he mustered before Bonnie pushed the painting aside, wrapped her leg around his waist and began to kiss his full lips in a vicious passion. He surrenders to her spell with little hesitation. Their bodies collide, breathes stammer, fingers dance off flesh.

Suddenly the wooden door violently jolts open to Jim, an angry white Mississippi man. "God dammit I told ya'll rat niggers to stay away from my wife. Unhand her!" With nothing more than a cigarette in his mouth and putrid disgust, Jim shoots a hole through the man's ribcage.

He falls over the canvas, blood and paint a seamless spectacle, a dreamy collage. Jim clutches Bonnie by the arm, dragging her out of the barn nestled within their garden.

No one remembers the Negro.

No one save the maid, who later in tears found his painting under dirt and straw. She marked the initials J.D. Tucker on the masterpiece she knew would change the world.

IF HEAVEN HAS PARTIES

Kaylie Meek

He's pretty sure you're supposed to die when this sort of thing happens. And then he looks down at the body at his feet and realizes yeah, actually, he did. Is that really what he looks like? Ben hopes he looked better without the blood and bones sticking out of his skin – and is that brain gunk leaking from his head? He turns from his mangled body to the disaster behind him – he'd been thrown clear from the car, and the distance was pretty impressive if he said so himself. The two cars are mangled heaps now, fluids leaking, glass everywhere. Ben hopes everyone else was okay.

The party at the Halliwell's house was the place to be that Saturday night. Some song was playing, Ben didn't know what; only that it was so loud his own thoughts got drowned out. Everywhere around him there were people dancing – was that Tanya Black without her top on? – and having a good time. Ben wove his way through the crowd, swaying to the beat (yes that was Tanya without her top on), making his way into the less crowded kitchen. Chips littered the tiled floor and the marbled counters, along with countless empty beer bottles, coke bottles, water bottles. It was a disaster, but it gave him space to think.

Perhaps it was a half-eaten chip or the way he set his drink down on the counter, but the thought burst into Ben's head *ohshitwhattimeisit?* It was harder to pull his phone out of his pocket than it should have been, and way harder to press the little home button for the screen to light up with the ominous numbers: 11:14. Alexis said they'd leave by 11, better to be home by their 12 o'clock curfew, but Ben should have known she wouldn't keep track of time like she said. It took an eternity to find his sister in the thrumming crowd, her sequined top sparkling in the dark room. It was hideous, but it made her easier to find, and Ben was grateful for the loud music as he grabbed Alexis' arm and tugged her out of the crowd – his sister could shriek.

It was simple enough to show her the time on his phone, a look of pure "I-told-you-so" on his face. The pair left quickly, the cool night air a welcome relief from the stuffy house. Alexis stumbled on the lawn, giggling as they made their way to the car. Ben had to help her down from the curb and unlock the door, settling himself in the passenger seat as she started the car.

Alexis didn't shut up the whole drive, twittering about this guy and that; Ben couldn't care less. The car swerved, Alexis righted it, giggling. It swerved again, and this time bright headlights filled the car and Alexis didn't giggle when the huge truck slammed into them.

His sister is fine, Ben decides, peering into the car. She's bleeding a lot, but breathing. By next week, she'll be fine enough to go to the next Halliwell party, free of little brothers. Ben just hopes heaven has parties without the drinking.

A SECOND CHANCE

Chris Molina

As he stood on the balcony overlooking his
beautiful mansion's view of the ocean upon the
tallest hill in Los Angeles, the greedy man was still
unsatisfied. To him, money came first above all other
things. He kept all his money to himself and would
flaunt it around the poor as entertainment. He got
pleasure out of this. The hardest part of his day was
choosing which $100,000 vehicle he should take for a
spin. After choosing the new black 2013 Audi r8, he
set out on the freeway. Feeling frustrated with this

"ordinary" vehicle, he sped up to push it to its limit. In an instant, he lost control and collided head on with another vehicle. When he regained consciousness, he looked around and saw his totaled car then laughed arrogantly and said, "What a worthless piece of shit, oh well, that's pocket change."

He was shocked to find he had not even one scratch on his body. He looked around and immediately noticed his surroundings did not appear normal. Complete darkness engulfed the freeway, and there was not a person or car in sight. Almost immediately his fear grew to panic, as he knew something wasn't right. He began walking away from the car and noticed a bright light in the distance. For an instant, he felt a sense of relief; he believed the light could lead to a way out.

But then, suddenly, as he drew closer to the light, the pungent smell of burning flesh rushed through his nostrils. Immediately looking up, he noticed an enormously large gate, and at the top of the gate were huge flaming letters, which spelled "GREED" and saw huge piles of burning money. As he heard piercing screams of agonizing pain; he shivered and shook as the realization of where he was suddenly struck him. Heat was radiating from his body; and momentarily, he felt his skin burning starting from his fingers then slowly spreading up to his arms. Soon the pain became so unbearable; he cried out in pain. It spread through his body until he could no longer withstand it. He wanted to die, but couldn't.

Screaming in agony, he woke at the scene of the accident abruptly. Breathing heavily, the man knew he was lucky to have escaped the fires of hell. As I oversee all of this from heaven I can only hope the greedy man will change his life after finding out that he ended mine.

A FAST HAND AND OVER-CONFIDENCE

Emilio Noriega

Powerful, heavy, weightless, destructive. The revolver was all of these things and more to me. It was always at my side, ready to fire whenever I needed it to. It was connected to my survival just as much as food and water were, plain and simple. It was heavy on my hand, however it was weightless on my soul. Maybe I should feel something for all of the people I've killed. Unfortunately, I don't. Some nights I would whirl the revolver around my finger and watch the embers of my campfire endlessly dance and crackle into the sunrise. Visions of duels filled my thoughts and the burn of hot metal could be felt in my palm, heck I could even almost smell the gunpowder. I suppose not much else was to be expected from the fastest hand in the West.

We stood apart at twenty paces, locked in an unbreakable stare. My hand was at the hip, tingling and twitching with anticipation. Me and my trusty revolver had been the victors of twenty-five duels already, and number twenty-six was right on its way. Confidence was coursing through my veins probably even more so than my own blood. This sorry-ass across from me had the nerve to try and cheat me out of my winnings in a game poker I was in at the town saloon, he says I cheated. He must've never heard of me. As soon as the second dropped his handkerchief, I would fire a round off right through his throat and that would be the end of the matter. I fancied the hat he was wearing too. I thought it would go just fine with my new coat. The second finally dropped the handkerchief. My hand moved swiftly for my revolver. I was lightning-quick and I could see that I had beat my opponent. My finger pressed the trigger back and Click! No bullet came out, it was jammed. As soon as the realization dawned on me, a bullet whizzed into the right side of my neck. Blood squirted everywhere and pain seared through every inch of my body. The revolver was in my left and my right hand covered the wound. My hand was warm and covered with blood. All I could do was stare at my revolver. It had failed me. "How ironic" I thought, "so, so ironic".

I began to lose my balance and my surroundings were becoming fuzzy. As the light began to fade from my eyes, I felt myself begin to fall into darkness. Falling, falling, endlessly into the dark abyss.

CRIMSON

Keaton Patterson

It was like throwing paint into a fan; all too soon did Rachel realize the severity of her actions. The hallways quickly flooded with students, all of them eager to see the truthful monstrosity she had created, that she had exposed. Karen Miller walked into school Monday morning to see a cluster of chaos; she pushed through the swarm of students and made her way forward, her curiosity getting the better of her, until she came to see what the commotion was about. Slut, whore, lesbian and skank were written across her locker in red paint and in a moment,

Karen Miller retreated into a cave as dark as the crimson red that scrolled her truth, that exposed her secret.

Karen Miller was new at Westview High; her dad had been moved down south for work. Though disappointed to be leaving everything she knew behind, Karen made the best of it. Her first few days were rough, but she had expected that. A few students had decided to take her under their wing, but quickly got bored of their pet project and slowly drifted. It was a Thursday when they first met. Rachel Jenkins was a junior, president of student congress and editor of the school newspaper, the Westview Inquirer. She had long blond hair and quick eyes the color of emerald green. The two girls made eye contact as they passed each other in the hallway, both lingering a little longer than normal. Over the course of a few weeks the two girls became fast friends and Karen was beginning to feel good about her place at west view.

A couple weeks later, a Saturday, the two girls

were painting posters for the homecoming pep rally in the cafeteria. They had spent the whole afternoon doing so and were the last ones there. When it was time to leave Karen helped Rachel take all the supplies to the custodial closet. The closet was cramped and only just big enough for the two girls to squeeze inside as they put back the paint brushes. Rachel glanced over to see Karen bend over and try to pick up a box that was obviously too heavy for one to carry alone. Rachel reached over to help, and in that moment their eyes locked. The two both close in proximity could feel their breath on each other's skin and Karen began to feel very hot. Rachel at that moment leaned in and kissed Karen, their lips tingled and Karen could not tell how much time had passed. Their breath became staggered and their bodies intertwined. Karen began to lean away but Rachel's grip became tight and, in that moment Karen pushed Rachel away and got out of the closet. Rachel apologized and told her she was confused, her eyes instantly flooding with tears as she panicked Karen grabbed her things and left without a word as Rachel sunk to the closet floor, her sobs broke. Karen looked back only once to see the green eyes that once were a striking emerald were now green with envy and fear. Rachel retreated into a cave as dark as the crimson red paint that filled her brush. It would no longer be only her secret the bare.

WHEN ONE DOOR CLOSES

Morgan Patterson

His hand rests on the doorknob, unsure. Leaving will undoubtedly break her heart. It will break his, too, if there is anything left of it to break.

Mark remembers falling in love with her, but then, he never really stopped. He smiles, thinking how she used to make everything so easy, effortless almost. The way she could make him laugh at anything, even at himself – that's how he knew she was the one.

They never laugh anymore. Mark grips the doorknob a little tighter, readjusts the bag on his shoulder. When planning what to pack for a life without Shelly, Mark found very little important enough to take along. Everything reminds him of her, and you can't start over by staring at the past. He fools himself though; there won't be any starting over, not this time.

Mark's resolve falters, and the doorknob starts to shake, just a little, under the weight of his hand. Shelly was so excited the day she told him about the baby, their baby. Mark was excited too, but the excitement didn't come until later. Fear came first. He didn't know how to be a dad. His own had been a poor example.

It didn't last long, though. Once the baby started growing inside her belly, Shelly positively glowed, and her joy was contagious, ushering out all of Mark's anxiety – there wasn't room for negativity anymore. He would lie at night, sometimes, with his head on her stomach and listen. Shelly wasn't far enough along for him to actually hear the baby's heartbeat, but he liked to pretend.

Shelly's voice drifts from the nursery, singing what should be a sweet, safe song, and Mark's bag drops to the ground, suddenly too heavy. She's always so sad now. This time he doesn't know how to make it better. Blinking the doorknob back into view, Mark tries not to see the baby's face. Mark doesn't want to see his baby's face. He lets go of the doorknob and walks into the next room. It is bright and pink, apart from the shadow that is his wife, empty and alone. He kneels in front of her as she rocks back and forth, humming the lullaby their daughter will never hear. And he cries.

No, he can't start over. That door closed forever.

LINDSEY'S BOOK

Ben Stiver

Her dad, searching curiously, next reached down into to the second drawer and found a small, magenta notebook hiding halfway beneath a calculator and a sociology textbook. At first glance, it figured to be he was looking for.

I don't understand what's so funny about crutches. A lot of people have to use them, why do they have to make fun of me for it? Its not very nice to call someone a loser, or a crippled. I wouldn't say any of this to them if one of them broke a leg.

I wish one of them had a broken leg, or really

anything that hurt them. It's been two weeks and they don't stop. I just have the dumb boot helping me walk but they still make fun of me. Except now they can't make fun of me for the crutches so they just like to call me names. They call me stupid, and I think I heard one call me a bitch, but I just try to ignore it. I thought they would have stopped by now.

I cried just yesterday. One of them called me a slut, and then told me I should leave the school. I don't even have anything wrong with me anymore! Why can't they just leave me alone! Out of the corner of my eye I think I might have seen Brittany, one of my good friends, let out a little laugh when they said it. Well, I probably just saw it wrong. I want to talk to my parents, but they won't understand, and my sister would try, but I know she just cares more about her stupid boyfriend.

The father turned the page, and the top right corner read March 24, just one week before today.

They are never going to stop saying all these things. As long as I am at this school life is going to suck. I cry almost every day now.

And with that Lindsey's father could read no further. He sat down and stayed there for a very long time. He looked around at the purple painted room with Lindsey's pictures strewn across the walls, happy smiles draping the faces of all of the picture's occupants. Pictures were a lie, and he was never going to take another again. At the end of that thought, Lindsey's father slowly rose to his feet, and started walking aimlessly away. But first, he dropped the diary on the bed that would now be absent of his baby girl forever.

IN THE STUDIO

Zach Tate

Her dream was finally coming true, being in front of the microphone, in the studio. She was doing what she does best. All the long nights with no sleep, just producing lyrics and getting that tone she needed to make her songs sound beautiful. Daisy stood behind the sound-proof glass, ready to sing her heart out on the machine, about to produce her first album.

As she was her vocals do the work, doing what she loved, she knew all her hard work was paying off. She was singing the lyrics she spent countless hours making. In the middle of singing her biggest hit she started thinking about her words, why she wrote it, and how she got the idea. Then it hit her, her songs were about one thing. The man from her hometown. She grew up with this handsome gentlemen, always singing to him and spent her days around him. As her fame got to her head, Daisy left him, without even saying goodbye, telling him that he wasn't the one, and she wasn't into him. She realized she has done the wrong thing, she left the person who cared about her the most, her biggest supporter. In the middle of her song, she suddenly stopped. She then dropped to her knees, and sat in despair. She was in shock and couldn't believe what she has done. She was in love with him all along. She blinded herself by the fame and fortune and forgot about the most important person in her life. Daisy slowly lifted herself up and walked over to her manager and producer and told her that this wasn't the place she should be. She walked out of the studio, with no regret, not even taking a slight look back and got on the first plane back home to where she belonged.

GLASS EYE

Samantha Gabrielle Thompson

I first saw the shadowy creature out of the corner of my eye, the false one, perched atop the shoulders of an old man buying two six-packs at the Shell station where I worked. I was still adjusting to blinking and the right lid had closed before the left and just for a split second I saw the hideous thing digging into his scalp. He winced slightly. Considering the fact that I can't see with that eye, it follows that I can't hallucinate with it either. Actually up until a few months ago it was just an empty space that kids on road trips would indiscreetly whisper about before their polite suburban mothers shushed them. I'd grown weary of watching the customers dance uncomfortably around the subject, and messing with them had become more morbid than entertaining, so I saved up for a perfect little blown glass copy of my right eye.

I checked the old man out, and took my break early. I put a cigarette to my mouth, lit the tip, and inhaled the smoke straight into my brain. About fifteen minutes passed and I was on my third menthol: finally calm enough to investigate what had happened. I closed both eyes slowly. and brought an unsteady hand to cover the right eye. I opened the left and saw. I actually fucking saw: my shitty car in the back of the store, the black gum stuck to the sidewalk, the flies hovering over the trashcans, and a couple arguing by the gas pumps. I walked toward the raised voices and saw more of the creatures from earlier surrounding the fight. Two on either side of the man seemed to egg him on, motioning violently toward the woman. The woman had three leech-like shadows clinging to her chest, seeming to suck her dry as tears streamed down her worn face. The couple didn't seem to notice the shadows, and as the screaming grew louder one of the figures grabbed the man's arm and raised it up high, bringing it down so hard that the woman fell to the dirty ground, hitting her head on the asphalt. The shadow leeches circled the pool of blood forming around her cracked skull. She would not get up. A heavier figure climbed onto the man's back. Like an anchor it pulled him down to his knees and his soul sunk into the darkest depths of grief.

I uncovered my right eye. Between the station and my apartment I finished off the rest of the menthols. On the nine o'clock news they talked about the old man who bought the six-packs at the station to wash down two pill cocktails, then the woman at the station, now dead, and the man who would have faced charges of murder had it not been for the pistol he placed gently in his mouth, the trigger he pulled gingerly, and the bullet that sped eagerly though the back of his tortured cranium.

What had I seen? What more would I see? I poured whiskey over rocks, lit my cigarette, sipped slowly, left the butt burning in the ashtray, then walked to the back of the closet feeling for the dusty rope necklace I'd tied years ago for a night like this. I secured the line to a support beam in the middle of the apartment and stood on my grandfather's rickety old chair. With my right eye covered I kissed goodnight the creature that I had carried on my shoulders for so long and waved goodbye to the one on my side as it kicked the chair out from under me.

CONTROL

Wesley Wilkinson

Even wearing my helmet made of precious tin foil someone carelessly left in the trash, I can hear their voices in my head. They know I can hear them, but they don't know that I know they're trying to control me. I can see them. They don't know I see them, but I see them. They are always watching me. I know they are. I see one now. A little one they just started training, I think. He pretends to wave at me but I can see he's trying the "hand force" technique to break the mental protection barriers of my helmet. The other trainees I've seen have better technique with the movement, but this one is wild with it. His sloppiness bothers me. His loudness aggravates me. I was instantly aware of his presence when he entered the doctor's office (where I am usually called a "Skits-o Frenchman" by a doctor that says I need help) and knew he was sent to turn me as soon as we met eyes. He looked too relaxed, almost happy to face me. I managed to show no fear.

I could see the child's movements becoming even wilder and could hear him growing even louder. He kept rambling on about "shots" and "needles". Maybe so that I wouldn't be suspicious of his true intention. But I'm smarter than that. His two trainers were starting to become aware that I was aware of his intention and tried quieting him. Nurturing him it seemed. The pathetic display the trainee was showing made me sick, so I decided to stop it. I stood up, walked to him and told him, "You are pathetic. If this is the best you can do then you should quit while you have the chance. Next time you trying to attack me I will kill you."

The trainee tried a new, almost impressive, tactic. He tried to make poison water (that I know only affects me) shoot at me from his eyes, but it just dripped down his face. He looked scared. The male trainer stood up, swung his fist towards me and then it was dark. But they still hadn't got to me.

They put me in a place with more "Skits-o Frenchmen" (and women). We plot now. When they aren't looking. They think we think we can't get out, but we know that they don't know we can. Soon we will escape. Soon we will be in control.

6395195R10044

Made in the USA
San Bernardino, CA
08 December 2013